Mister Negative and Other Stories

Robert Peate

Contact Robert Peate at rpeate@gmail.com.

Published by Truth Tales, Portland, Oregon

Printed in the United States of America

ISBN-13: 978-1475204483
ISBN-10: 1475204485

Also by Robert Peate:

The Recovery
Visits with Catholicism

The Gentle Tara Tales

Gentle Tara and the Butter-Fly Ride
Gentle Tara and the Haunted House
Gentle Tara and the Bloodstone Locket
Gentle Tara and the Wizard War

Praise for *Mister Negative and Other Stories*

"Chasing Kerouac"

"I wouldn't change a word. It is a perfect story."

—Dana Ross

"I like historical fiction and reads that describe a location so perfectly that you just know it exists. I want to see the torn-up bathroom."

—Cyndi Bowdish Noyes

"Mister Negative"

"I haven't laughed so hard—and so consistently—at a piece of prose since *Catch-22*."

—Keanu Allridge

"Because every party needs a pooper."

—Megan Clark Stonic

Praise for *The Recovery*

"A great read. He [Robert Peate] presents a very plausible alternative to the 'miracle' story of Jesus's resurrection and his distaste for what became of his legacy. . . . I wish every middle or high school would put on this play for their Easter pageant."

—Dana Ross

"It certainly will throw some of the straight-laced into an uproar. (Being the kind of person I am, I sometimes enjoy throwing the straight-laced into an uproar.)"

—Bill Sifferle

"This is the kind of fiction that shakes people up. It challenges them right down to the core, which in my opinion is how things should be. My son's response was, 'This will piss some people off.' But he sees the possibility of truth in the fiction."

—Cyndi Bowdish Noyes

Praise for *Gentle Tara and the Butter-Fly Ride*

"It flows. You have a nice poetic feel to your fiction writing without sacrificing realistic dialogue."

—Joy Clines

"As with every one of Robert's works I was very pleasantly surprised at how much I enjoyed this book. A thoughtful and well thought out book, I found it a wonderful escape and charm to read as I followed the adventures of Gentle Tara and her friends, both human and magical. I believe that anyone and everyone who enjoys discovering the world through the eyes of a child will love this book."

—Chuck Weiss

"WONDERFUL!"

—Kym Tuvim

"For me it's a book that I will read with my grandkids when I get them."

—Cyndi Bowdish Noyes

Praise for *Gentle Tara and the Haunted House*

"Very Cute Ghost Story."

—Joy Clines

Table of Contents

If you find me shocking
then you need to get out more.

—Sharon Hoffman

I never give them Hell.
I just tell the truth and they think it's Hell.

—Harry Truman

Introduction "Chasing Kerouac"

December 5+, 2010
Gualo Rai, Saipan

The following story, written in August of 2008, was inspired by a graduate class I had taken the previous spring in preparation for becoming an English teacher, American Fiction III, from the 1950s to the present. This course included Jack Kerouac, and for the class we read *The Dharma Bums* (1958). Over the following summer, I read half of *On the Road* (1957) out of a sense of obligation. I felt that Kerouac was a bit of a charlatan (certainly not the most demanding of himself as a writer), though his spontaneous approach was novel. I found his work more valuable historically than aesthetically.

That summer I also continued a creative relationship with novelist, screenwriter, and Portland State University professor Charles Deemer I had begun the summer before. While working with him on his Small-Screen Video project, in which I acted in short films shot on a Flip Video Mino Camcorder, I learned that he had published a novel entitled *Kerouac's Scroll* (Sextant Press, 2006), about two men who drive across the United States to view the original 120-foot teletype scroll of *On the Road*, created in April 1951, on display at the Smithsonian Institution. The title gave me the idea of a "lost" scroll, and who doesn't like a treasure hunt? I took Charles' form ("two men on a car trip to see a Kerouac scroll") and twisted it to revolve around a different idea. To alter that form sufficiently (and provide the rationale for the search), I took the opportunity to parody Kerouac's fanatical admirers—lovingly, of

12

course. Only a passionate hunter would drive hundreds of miles to track such a quarry as a piece of paper.

In Kerouac's defense, I will say that he was a good writer. Not a great one, but a good one. His greatness was obstructed, perverted by Catholicism. Am I the only one who can see the greatness in others that *might have been*? I hope not.

Jack Kerouac was very perceptive, and he excelled at recording his perceptions, hence his historical value. But he gave insufficient attention to the *craft* of writing, to plot structure, to considering his audience. He blasts the reader and says, "Play catch-up!" No, thank you.

In my opinion, his writing is literary vomit. Because his tone is "serious" and his subjects are earthy, his dysfunction and carelessness are overlooked, considered "style". His voice is garbled.

One criticism I received, from my old friend Kevin Babcock, reflected this (you might want to save reading it until after reading the story):

> . . . I thought you were rather quick to develop characters and scenes. You could easily take a few more pages to describe individuals and to develop dialogue. For example, in "Kerouac" the woman from the cabin just comes right out and propositions the guy out of the blue. The reader was prepared for a lengthy discussion from these two, for her explanation of how few people come

by this way, some flirtation, some come-ons perhaps, and then her cornering of this stranger for the big question. It was like you envision the scene for yourself and sort of fast forward to spare the reader minute details that distract from the story when that is exactly the kind of raw human emotion they may have been expecting and so sort of feel rushed when the scene concludes with such little development. It's like, "Whoa, how did we get here?" I hope you understand where I am coming from and don't assume I am telling you how to write. I am telling you how I felt at that point in the story. I felt you could have easily embellished on many points in this book and it wouldn't at all feel like you were dragging or running on just to fill pages. The reader is eager for the content, and it felt like you were sparing them and getting right to the point. Don't spare us. Write down every detail, no matter how insignificant, and you can always cut it out later. Personally I want more from a good writer, not less. I know how to skim over the shite when I read it.

And this is a good example of a strong and reasonable criticism. It is true I am an economist with words (my wife laughs when I say that), or at least that I tend to skim over the signifiers to plant seeds in the mind without dwelling too long on a given one. I want the reader's imagination to have the freedom to roam on its own. That is a general statement.

In this case, I made the decision—well, I'll let my response to Kevin speak for itself:

> Re: the scene with Anya and Scott: one of my subtle visions in writing the story was to engage in a meta-Kerouac style. In other words, Kerouac's stories are filled with crazy characters doing inappropriate things. That was an intentional nod to that kind of absurdity, which is a fancy way of saying, "I meant to do that." But I am telling the truth.

I wanted the reader to be reminded of a Kerouac story by my own. Of course I understand he or she won't always be, whether due to never having read Kerouac or my not being an effective writer.

Maybe I was *too* subtle, but "Whoa, how did we get here?" is exactly the reaction I wanted, as that is exactly the reaction Kerouac causes on most pages. It's another statement on Kerouac. I take Kevin's response above as confirmation of my success.

Amazingly, one person with whom I shared this story said my Kerouac paragraphs did not sound like

Kerouac. I say "amazingly" because I based both of them on a specific paragraph in *On the Road*, merely changing details. I could only laugh and assume the person was not as familiar with Kerouac as he had wished *me* to believe he was.

That said, I am Peate, not Kerouac. The paragraphs are "Peate does Kerouac", not "Kerouac". But I am satisfied that they are close enough.

For those who care what I think, I consider this the most perfectly-structured story I have ever written. When I read it, I can hardly believe I wrote it. I love it.

"Chasing Kerouac"

"I'm telling you, there's a lost scroll!" Dean Tucker insisted to me. "It's mentioned only in passing, in the January 1957 *Steve Allen Show* interview. Kerouac clearly states that he's finished a short story, but that he isn't satisfied with it. 'For fun,' he says, 'I hid it in the wall of my friend Bill's bathroom. Let future excavators come across it and marvel.' Then he takes out a cigarette and never mentions it again. Most historians take that line as a joke, but I tell you, it's there!"

"On what do you base that?" I asked him with the courtesy of someone who is tired of the topic.

"His schedule. For the entire year of 1956, there is a record of everything he wrote except for the month of September—when he suddenly goes silent, picking up again with *The Lords of Chicago*. There is no explanation for the silence, in the middle of his most fertile and creative period, except that he wrote the most famous piece of his that no one has ever read!" Dean glowed, triumphant.

"It's an intriguing theory," I conceded. "But who was this 'Bill'? Where did he live?"

Dean was prepared for my question, pulling a folded map from his pocket. "I have a map." Unfolding just enough of it to show me the relevant area, he smoothed it with his hands. "Up outside of Yosemite National Park, this is where Kerouac went to recuperate after he caught the flu that August. It's the only explanation that makes sense, and I can't understand why no one else has figured this out before." He shook his head with sincere rue.

"Maybe no one else is as crazy, or 'dedicated', as you," I offered in an attempt to be helpful.

"You're probably right. Kerouac is my life," Dean nodded.

"Well, I think you've solved the mystery," I said. "Now someone will just have to find the scroll someday."

"We leave tomorrow," Dean said. "I've already packed the car."

"What?"

"It's Friday tomorrow. You don't work again until Tuesday. We can go there, find the story, and be back here by Monday night."

"You are insane—I'm not breaking and entering!"

"It's for literature! Even if we get caught, we'll be heroes!"

"We'll be locked up!"

"Won't it be glorious?"

"I'm not going."

"Aw, come on."

I couldn't say no to my best friend, in the end.

"What's the name of this story?" I asked the next morning, bleary-eyed, not really caring, as we got ready.

"No one knows," Dean said, "not even his mother. That's what makes the mystery so exciting."

I couldn't help but notice that, even at six in the morning, Dean was as awake as ever. We had a long day of driving south from Portland, Oregon, ahead, but all he could think about was this holy grail of Kerouac's. I was still convinced it didn't exist. Everyone knew that Kerouac liked a good joke, and that he was capable of spinning yarns at will. Maybe he took September 1956 off to smoke dope with Allen Ginsberg or Gary Snyder in the mountains? But I couldn't begrudge Dean his excitement. It mattered a great deal to him. Kerouac had been his hero all his life.

A short time later we found ourselves in Dean's beat up 1991 Nissan Sentra, loaded for bear, heading south on I-5 toward Salem, Oregon. "This is crazy," I said, as I started to wake up.

"Nah. It's fun. Worst-case scenario, we don't find the story, but we have a good time." I took this as a rare moment of rationality from Dean.

"Worst-case scenario we get arrested for burglary," I couldn't help saying.

It was a hot day in July, and we drove with the windows down, as Dean's air conditioning was long busted.

After driving all day that Friday, with the usual pit stops, we made it to Eureka, California, that night. After supper at a bad Indian place, I argued for stopping, but Dean was too excited. He wanted to continue.

"I'm too tired," I said. "I can handle long drives, even not eating, but I can't handle not sleeping well. I get cranky," I warned. "You won't want me burgling in that state." He seemed to take that seriously, so we stopped at the cheapest motel we could find, a pink-painted dive named the Flamingo, with bullet holes in our room door and graffiti on the furniture.

"Wow," I said as we walked in. "This place is straight out of Kerouac."

"Now you're getting the spirit! Feel his ghost passing through you," Dean enthused, and I wasn't sure if he meant it figuratively or literally.

I was still dubious about the existence of this supposedly "lost" story, but I didn't mind humoring Dean. Named after the character Dean Moriarty in *On the Road*, he had spent his life in the shadow of Kerouac, immortalizing him, worshiping him. Who was I to shatter, or otherwise hinder, his illusions? So, with Dean's parents to thank, we found ourselves on the road, chasing Kerouac.

The next day, Saturday, we continued south to San Francisco, then turned east to Stockton, Modesto, and Merced, on the road to Yosemite. We drove straight up into the mountains, where we knew Kerouac and Snyder had hiked, backpacked, and visited "Wild Zane of the Mountain". This mysterious, semi-legendary figure was rumored not even to be real, since no photographs of him existed. Cynics said Jack, Gary, Allen, and others made him up to create an excuse for their excursions into the forest when others disapproved. Dean was a believer. I was apathetic. Dean whipped out his map as we approached the roads on it. The gravel under his tires crunched as we drove off the highway, the Sun beating down on both of us.

"Try not to be too disappointed when we don't find anything," I said. It was a slip, an accidental violation of my own internal promise not to harm his pleasure.

"You try to have more faith!" he said. "Remember, Kerouac was raised Catholic."

"Yes, yes, he was," I said. My own personal hypothesis was that Kerouac's Catholicism caused him a lifetime of self-loathing and alcoholism over having been bisexual, and that faith in destructive concepts or attitudes was contrary to Kerouac's own stated ambitions. Of course, in this case, Dean's faith in a lost manuscript couldn't be too destructive . . . could it? I looked at Dean, tried to evaluate how he would react if he didn't find his holy grail, and decided he'd be able to handle it. He was rational enough to know it was probably long gone, eaten by termites, or bulldozed with Bill's house. We didn't even know if the house was still standing. Come to think of it, we didn't know if this house, or the friend named Bill, wasn't just another product of Kerouac's eternally spinning imagination. I had odds, placed silently to myself, that we would go back home that day or the next, defeated and dejected, but wiser.

"Right here," Dean said, studying his map carefully. We had been taking turns driving, and it happened that I was the driver at that point. I offered to let him drive the last leg of our exciting journey of discovery, but he quickly shook his head no, saying he would much rather read the map. "Keep going straight until we come to another fork, then turn left."

We followed the network of narrower and narrower gravel roads, until they became dirt with deep tire tracks akin to gullies, and I began to wonder how Jack Kerouac, Gary Snyder, or anyone else ever found his way here. But the tire tracks proved someone had.

We came upon a small brown shack by the side of the road on the right, and we stopped and got out to ask directions. Then we noticed the house was so run down it didn't seem possible anyone could live there. A name on the mailbox read, "Carlson". Dean puzzled over this.

"I seem to remember in an interview, or story, or article . . . Kerouac mentioning a Carlson girl . . . I think we're on the right track!" Dean jumped back in the car. "Come on! It's not much farther now." I slowly walked back to the car door, opened it, and got in.

"It's not long now!" Dean said. "Aren't you excited?"

"Yes," I said. "Your enthusiasm is infectious."

"Even if you don't care about the story, it will be a significant literary discovery, which will make us famous," Dean offered by way of compensation for my participation in the journey.

"I want to be famous for my own writing, not someone else's," I countered. In a way, Dean's sycophantic love of all things Jack Kerouac made me sick. But then, didn't I have my idols? I did, but I told myself they were different, or at least that I was different in regard to them. Somehow. Perhaps it was that I simply didn't share his idolatry. Idolatry in common can be blissful, but when it is not shared, idolatry can be tedious.

We drove a little longer. "We should be able to see Bill's house after we clear the next rise . . . ," Dean said, his voice fading as his mind switched resources from his voice to his vision. We cleared the next rise, and saw a little cottage set apart from the road, on the left. "That's it," Dean whispered.

The cottage looked lived in, its faded blue paint chipping and cracking, grass overgrown, a dead old tractor on the other side. The driveway was empty.

We stopped and got out. "They'll probably be nervous, so let me do the talking," Dean said.

"Funny, I was thinking they'd probably be nervous so I should do the talking," I bantered back. "I mean, you're a lunatic."

"Ha, ha."

A young, tired woman in a cleaning apron answered the door. "Hello," said Dean.

"Hello," said the woman, her hair matted with perspiration, leaning on a broom.

"Are you aware that you are living in the former home of a friend of the twentieth century's greatest literary genius, Jack Kerouac, the creator of 'spontaneous writing'?"

The woman seemed neither to know nor to care. Trying again, Dean said, "There is the possibility that a literary work of great value is hidden in your house. May we look for it? That's why we've driven for two days from Portland."

"You can talk to my husband when he gets home from work," she said. She gave us a suspicious look. "After seven."

"Thank you, Ma'am," I said. "Let's go, Dean." I grabbed his arm and tugged. We walked back to the car. Though the afternoon was lengthening, it was still hot out. "We can go back down the road and get dinner."

"Dinner? How can you think of food at a time like this?" He was shocked at the idea of leaving this sacred place, in case the holy grail would get away from its bathroom wall in the few hours before the husband returned home.

"We can't stay here. The woman already thinks we're freaks. We have to leave, or she'll call the police." I could have been wrong, but I had to stress to him our need to appear reasonable.

"You're right," he said suddenly, casting a look back at the house, a look filled with friendly joviality. "Let's go."

Whew, I thought.

We talked about it over supper at a diner back on the main road, thirty minutes down through the mountains. "Clearly, that woman is insane. Did you see the look on her face? Or she thought we were insane," I said.

"Perhaps a little of both. But we're getting close—I can feel it! I can feel there is something here."

"Maybe we should go look for that mountain man—Old Zane, was it? If he exists, he might know about it."

"You just want to get away from this house," Dean accused.

"You're right—that woman gave me the Willies. Her husband is probably some big lumberjack who'll kill us on sight."

"Come on, Scott. Where's your sense of adventure?"

"I left that behind with roller coasters as an adolescent. I like playing it safe now. It keeps me alive. And well."

"Well, not me. I want into that bathroom wall, and I'll do almost anything to get into it."

"You're the crazy one." I bit into my hamburger and said no more about it.

That night the husband thought it a great idea to open the wall. "We'll do it tomorrow. I'm off then, and it's too late to start tonight. It'll be dark out shortly, and impossible for searching." He said he had read *On the Road* years before, so knew something of Kerouac. "You really think there's a piece of Kerouac behind our bathroom tile?" he asked Dean, as his wife looked on skeptically, haggard.

"Yes, I do. I know my friend Scott here thinks I'm crazy, but I do." I said nothing, but rolled my eyes to reveal that I did, in fact, think his enthusiasm was a bit irrational.

The master of the house, an older man with bushy grey hair, a beard, and a plaid flannel shirt, of the Viet Nam generation, had introduced himself as Reddy Marx when we arrived. After we secured his agreement, I felt we should leave Reddy and his younger wife to their evening. Dean and I would need to find another motel, hopefully one better than the Flamingo. "We should go," I said. "We need to find lodging."

"Don't be silly!" Reddy said. "You can have our room. Anya and I've already discussed it. And if you get the urge to break through the bathroom wall during the night, I don't suppose I can stop you."

"Well, this is an unexpected pleasure!" I said, extremely suspicious. *He wants to rob or kill us*, I couldn't help thinking. At first I thought he'd get rid of us out the door so he could look for the manuscript himself. Then I thought his motives even more sinister. "But we don't want to be any trouble to you," I finished, giving Dean a significant look of, "Let's not stay here."

Dean was too excited. "Scott, they've just extended their hospitality," he said in front of them. "It would be rude to decline. Besides, if you feel uncomfortable, you can sleep out in the car." We both knew that was not an option—the car was filled with his rucksack and other gear. Sleeping outside under the Stars, à la Kerouac and Ryder, suddenly seemed preferable to me.

"Fine," I said, feeling very bad about this, my inner New Yorker highly skeptical of these odd hosts.

The night passed uneventfully. Reddy and Anya were up late, but I was up later, sitting in the dark on the bed as Dean snored, watching the light crack under the door, expecting them to attack us any minute. I sat upright another hour after the light went out, finally falling asleep about three. I knew Dean would be waking about four anyway; he usually did, being jumpy. When I dragged myself out of bed about eight, Dean, Reddy, and Anya were already studying the bathroom tile.

"Did you find it?" I asked sleepily. "May I use the bathroom?" They had been engrossed in their tile analysis, but, startled back to courtesy, ceased and stepped aside for my sake.

"There's coffee left over," Anya offered. It was the first kind sentence she'd uttered.

"Thank you!" I said, and gently closed the bathroom door.

Dean's entire life had been spent in anticipation of this moment. He was not actually very much like his namesake; my Dean was more quiet, scientific, and introverted, not so much a womanizing car thief. He took out his notes, and concluded, "There is nothing specific. We have to tear it all out, unless we can figure out which tiles may have been open or loose in the 'Fifties.'" He searched the tiles pleadingly, hoping they would give him an answer. And they did. In one corner, he noticed a discoloration, what seemed to be a mismatched tile. "Could it have been broken and replaced?" Dean asked Reddy.

"Anything's possible," Reddy said. "Might as well smash it, since we're considering smashing all the rest anyway." He produced a hammer and began hitting the tile. It cracked, then fell apart. Reddy stuck his hand in. "I think I've got it!" And he had: it was too easy, almost. But he had found a rolled-up parchment, fastened with an old rubber band, typed in the unmistakable font of an old typewriter. This was pre-Apple Pages, pre-Microsoft Office Word, or even WordPerfect, to be sure.

"Amazing," Dean uttered. The rest of us gathered around Reddy in the cramped bathroom. We had to see it for ourselves to believe it. Reddy was leaning farther and farther backward over the toilet bowl as we crowded against him.

"Let's go to the living room," Reddy said, supporting himself against the back wall. We made straight for it.

"This is an amazing discovery, as Dean said," Reddy said. "As owners of the property on which it was found, we have some rights." I foresaw a huge haggle, fight, and pain.

"What do you intend to do with it?" Anya asked us, primarily Dean.

"Get it published," Dean said. "I want the World to read it." Speaking of reading, none of us had even thought to open the scroll, we'd been so wrapped up in the simple excitement of discovering it. Reddy handed it to Dean, appreciating that even if he had rights, this was Dean's show. Dean touched the rubber band, which had grown brittle over fifty years behind a basement wall, and it crumbled into dust. He opened the paper, which seemed fairly long.

"I can hardly believe it," Dean said, tears forming in his eyes. "I've dreamed of this my whole life." He read aloud:

Quirky 'Querque

In my wanderings across our fair nation, I spent some time in the southwest working in an old gold mine for a week, helping some crazy grizzled prospector, Old Sparky, who insisted there was gold under the New Mexican mountains. It was the final parting gift of the ancient Indian gods, he'd say. After a week outside Las Cruces, Old Sparky and I parted ways, with no gold dust found. I didn't think he'd ever find anything. He paid me three dollars for my trouble and I was off. I thought about trying to find Terry again when I reached LA, but it had been years, and I was sure she'd settled down by then. She was just another fanciful dream.

I found myself in Albuquerque. I was dropped there by a friendly older couple, religious types, who hadn't felt the need to share with me the Good Lord's word, probably since they could tell I'd already heard it. It was a beautiful day. I stopped into a silver diner opposite the railroad tracks for a bite, possessed with the spirit of good fortune. Something had changed for the better, I could feel it. The first thing I did was have a fine coffee, strong enough to glue your toes together.

"This is . . . wonderful!" Dean exclaimed. "It's the lost adventure of Jack Kerouac!" He sat down. "It goes on—it's all about some people he met at this diner in Albuquerque. He gives character analysis . . . meets another girl . . . has a romance. Her father doesn't like it, chases Jack out of the house with a gun! He could have died!" Dean was overcome. "This makes everything else more meaningful! He hadn't written *The Dharma Bums* or *The Subterraneans* yet! Imagine if he'd been killed!"

"We'd all be sitting around thinking *On the Road* was all he had in him," I said. "All right, I was wrong. Let's go home and call publishers." I stood up.

"This calls for a celebration," Reddy said. He produced two bottles of wine and some beer. "We'll all be rich and famous." I felt that eight-thirty in the morning was a little early to start drinking, and was dubious, but Dean was delighted.

It turned out that Reddy was a poet who'd been waiting years for an audience, so he took this opportunity to give a reading, "in tribute to the Beat Generation". Before we could protest, he whipped out a sheaf of papers and began to read aloud.

"Ode to a Horse," he intoned. "This one is about my favorite childhood pet."

About two hours later, I excused myself to get some air, strolled out onto their humble porch and past it to the car. I stood at the driver's side door, wishing Dean were outside getting air with me, so I could pack him in the passenger side and go home. Anya came outside and saw me shuffling about in the dirt road.

"You haven't had breakfast yet," she said. "Come back in. I'll fix you something nice."

"No, thanks," I returned. "I'm fine." She kept coming toward me. After she had stepped around the car, she picked something off my shoulder.

"Reddy and I don't love anymore," she said. "It's been a long time since I've had the pleasure of a man's *full* company." As she made eyes at me, the breeze played with her hair, and her face looked more attractive than it had the day before. She placed her hands on both my shoulders and leaned in for a kiss.

"I'm sorry," I said, pulling back and disengaging her hands from my shoulders. (Luckily, I could still hear Reddy inside roaring away, about cars and trees and Life, even Dean shouting, "Yeah, yeah!") "I'm sorry for your troubles, but I'm spoken for," I lied, "and, whether happily or not, so are you." Her face soured.

"Reddy doesn't mind!" she said, making another attempt to sweet-talk me. For all I knew she was a serial killer. I stepped backward, New York nerves on alert. I had to get Dean and the scroll out of there. I went back inside, Anya following.

At the moment I stepped back in, Reddy had finished his sheaf of papers. "You all right, man? This is great stuff! You just missed the best one!" Dean inquired, exclaimed, and mourned, after clapping. I nodded my sorrow at having missed "the best one". "You got any more?" Dean sincerely asked Reddy.

"Do I!" enthused Reddy. "I'll be right back!" He went to the bedroom to rummage. Now was our chance. I grabbed "Quirky 'Querque" and pulled Dean up. He didn't have any other belongings to retrieve.

"We're going," I whispered.

"No!" Dean slurred. "It's just getting good!"

"It'll have to get good some other time." I dragged him outside by one arm past Anya, who smoldered and glowered at me.

"I'll tell my husband you made a pass at me!" she threatened. That was when I really knew it was time to leave—and that he would really mind his wife fooling around with other men.

"Have a good Sunday," I said. "Tell your husband we loved his poetry." I opened the passenger door and placed Dean inside his car as gently as I could, but his limbs, and his mind, didn't always cooperate. I could hardly believe he had allowed himself to become drunk before breakfast.

"Hey, man! Lemme outta here."

As fast as I could, I ran around to the other side of the car. Luckily, Dean's attempts to open the passenger door were hindered by his inebriation and his cradling the scroll more gently than a baby. He cursed me. At that moment, Reddy emerged from the house with another sheaf of papers.

"I got 'em!" he exclaimed proudly. "My set of 'honeymoon' poems! I wrote these when we went up to Bear Lake!" Reddy was tipsy himself, but not so much so that he didn't notice me starting the car to go, or Anya standing there with arms folded, tapping her foot in anger.

"What happened?" he asked, but it was too late. We were off.

"Hey," Dean moaned, his head falling to the side. "That's not nice. Where are we going, anyway?"

"Home," I said. "Fast." I just hoped the Marxes hadn't made a note of Dean's license-plate number.

"What about Wild Zane of the Mountain?" Dean asked as I drove as fast as I could, his car raising dust from the dirt road.

"We'll visit him next time," I said, concentrating on not getting stuck in a tire-gully. "That was wild enough for me."

Looking back, I saw Anya shaking her fist at us.

"We'll have to send her a card," I said.

A few hours later, Dean was sober, driving, and pensive, not speaking half as much as usual.

"Well? What is it?" I asked, turning to face him. "What's got you? We accomplished—*you* accomplished your lifelong dream. You were right when everyone else was wrong. You're going to be remembered forever as contributing to the history of American literature."

"Yes," Dean said grimly, still concentrating on something beyond the road beyond his steering wheel. "But now that it's found, what do I live for? What is there left to seek?" He looked at me then, doubt in his eyes.

"You live for you," I said. "Kerouac will live forever, and even more now, thanks to you. But you are alive here and now. Frankly, I think he'd trade places with you."

Dean nodded, slapped his steering wheel in imitation of Dean Moriarty, and said, "Whee! You're right!"

"That's the spirit," I smiled.

And we continued roaring down the road, driving all day and night for kicks. We found ourselves on the outskirts of Portland at eight o'clock the next morning, ravenous for breakfast. At Sully's in Milwaukie, we found it. I had their Mediterranean omelet, which I loved.

Soon afterward, "Quirky 'Querque" took its rightful place among all other Kerouac classics, even kindling interest in him in a new generation of readers, thanks to the buzz it produced in the media. We attended press conferences to announce the discovery and then the publication of the short story. Dean realized his lifelong dream. I was very glad for him. Even Reddy and Anya got their due, as reporters and tourists made regular pilgrimages to gaze at the

34

hole in their bathroom wall. They turned their home into a mini Kerouac tourist trap. Dean gave them a share of the publishing royalties as well.

We caught you, Jack.

With thanks to Charles Deemer for the inspiration and B. Marley (not Bob) for the good advice.

Introduction: "Neighbors"

December 5, 2010
Gualo Rai, Saipan

The following story, written on December 8 of 2009, was inspired by a neighbor in Portland, Oregon, who kept her children on what seemed to my wife and me to be too-short a leash. We felt sorry for the children, who were morose. Their mother, of course, wished to project perfection. The kids just wanted to be kids.

At times I would wonder what the incarcerated children did inside all day. Then I wrote this story, to entertain my own imagination to its logical conclusion, while accepting all the blame. I wanted to be wrong, after all.

"Neighbors" is another story that came out in a burst, but it is the only complete story I have written in one sitting. I just started and kept going, which was not only unusual for me but a unique, once-in-a-lifetime event. I didn't feel pressure, other than the belief that if I stopped I would never continue, as I had abandoned countless other "false starts" before. I should publish a book of my false starts entitled *Starts* and let Hollywood enjoy playing with my inspirations, my mental cast-off refuse, which it could easily do for decades, there are so many of them (including a veritably made-for-television police-drama dream I transcribed in the fall of 1990) . . . , but I won't. I will content myself to publish only completed works until such time that I publish my complete works.

In this story, I just kept pushing. When a crazy direction occurred to me, I knew I had to follow it, wherever it led. I did not know where it would lead, as I never know where my stories will lead until I write them, but I found this one's ending logical and satisfying—once it occurred. Writing is a matter of seeing events through to their logical conclusion once they have begun, which is why writing is hard.

To be clear: it is not the logic but the seeing through that is hard. Usually I'm just too lazy to write it down, once I see where it is going. In this case, I didn't see where it was going until I got there.

It surprises me to realize, looking back on some of these stories ("Chasing Kerouac" and "Neighbors"), that each is written in the first person, because we (or I) tend to admire most the third person omniscient, with its objectivity and omniscience. The first person would seem to be the opposite, and yet it is the most natural. Who should tell a story but a person? The pressure of setting oneself up as a god, aware of and relating all, is usually too great for me. It prevents storytelling. These stories slipped under that radar, were easier to tell as a result. I was able to select my own narrator's "voice", which aided the factual revelations to come. The personality of the narrator enabled his or her editorial commentary, which is out of the question in a third-person work. The narrator in that case must let his or her characters do the speaking for him or her—not completely, but more so. This is a constriction avoided by these stories, coincidentally. I spent years thinking that every "serious" story must be written in the third person, failing to appreciate that each story was different, requiring a different narrative voice that was suggested by its own needs, and that imposing the third person point of view (omniscient or not) on some stories would prove deleterious. In these cases, the humanity of the first person was required.

It also occurs to me that two of these recent stories were prompted by minor annoyances (Kerouac fanatics, a mysterious neighbor), and that other stories I have written in the past were prompted by crises. Evidently there's something to that advice about lemons.

38

"Neighbors"

One day over the summer Amber and her two children moved into the empty house next door to the south, one of several houses in our development that had been empty for months due to what they had started calling the Great Recession about the time it was ending, over the summer. Amber seemed peppy but distant, and we almost never saw her or her children, until one day we realized we really did never see them. The lights were sometimes on; Amber's vehicle was sometimes in the driveway; once my son and I interacted with Amber as she left one early morning; and once, before the summer ended, she came outside with her two children to photograph them playing, to give the impression to others, perhaps, that the activity was routine, but that was it.

What were they doing in there? More importantly, why did we never see them? Who would she try to persuade her children routinely played outside? They had lived there for at least three months when December came—not that we were keeping track, but they had definitely arrived over the summer. We understood it had become cool, so we didn't expect to see them outside very often, but . . . at least inside.

On the other hand, no one could see us inside our house either. We were probably being paranoid. It's not as if we had any idea of anything inappropriate they could be doing. We were just consumed by curiosity.

I didn't really want to spy on the neighbors through their windows at night, but I felt I owed it to the children. This was clearly a bad mother, and someone had to investigate. I didn't want to call the national child-abuse hotline without any sort of evidence, and everyone knows that abuse usually goes on in secret. It was my moral duty to assemble evidence for the eventual call to the hotline. I started sneaking into their back yard, so I could peer into their ground-floor living space, after supper, when I could assume the cold weather would prevent them from coming outside. It occurred to me that perhaps they had been playing outside in their back yard all along, instead of the side yard, but then we would have at least heard something. No; something was up.

I peered in to see Amber and her two children, a girl and a boy, watching television on their living-room sofa, *Medium*, *The Mentalist*, or something. Everything seemed normal. I knew I'd have to step up my research. She was starting to suspect me, I felt, so I would have to be both more sneaky and more invasive.

I bought some gear. Some special binoculars. I thought of asking a locksmith to make a wax mold of the front-door lock while Amber and family were away, but I decided not to do so, since I didn't have a key to the house, and he might ask me to open the door to show that I lived there. Also, he was a friend of mine, and he knew where I lived. It was too risky, but I did discuss my concerns about the woman and her family with with my friend.

"Why in Hell don't you leave this family alone?" he asked me. "They're just normal neighbors.

What they do in the privacy of their own home is none of your business."

"But it's suspicious," I said. "I don't want to break any laws, but I can't help worrying about those kids. They never play outside."

"It's December. For all you know, they go to a gym or community center for play and exercise." It was true that Amber was the athletic type, or at least she wore the clothes. Could that be it? Should I ask her about it? She might not have liked my questioning her habits, which is why I decided I would have to conduct my research clandestinely.

"Yeah, you're right," I said, and that was that. The rest of the visit until he left was a formality. While I didn't want to break any laws, I decided it was necessary. But I would have to work alone, not making the mistake of trying to enlist aid again. I began to research electronic listening devices. If I could plant one in her house, even her SUV, I could find out what she was doing to those poor kids. My wife began to question my behavior and purchases. I told her I was preparing a special photography project, and she demurred.

This took a lot of work. I did succeed in ordering some small listening devices, but I had to drill an unobtrusive hole in the wall of her house when all three of them weren't there. Speaking of three, where was her husband? When we'd met she said "we", referring to the father of her children and herself. I had never seen a man in the picture, though my wife had claimed to have seen one. Perhaps the man my wife saw was just a friend visiting once, a passing acquaintance, or even some stranger Amber had hired to deceive us. Why would she go to such lengths to deceive her new neighbors? For what nefarious project was she laying groundwork, preparing the neighborhood? At the same time that I began to install the bug, I visited the head of our Homeowner's Association—not to enlist him, but to express my concerns.

Ron was an elderly man, retired, but very observant and helpful about the housing development. I felt if anyone knew what was going on behind closed doors, it would be him. He received me cordially, and we talked.

"Well, I haven't had any complaints about her, Jeff—they've been very quiet, keeping to themselves."

"That's the problem. I think there's something going on there."

"Like what?"

"Ritual child abuse, even mutilation or murder."

"What?" he laughed. "You're crazy." He seemed about to offer me a drink.

"That's what they said about Rasputin," I said, brilliantly quoting Chevy Chase in *Caddyshack*. "Remember: 'Al Qaeda Determined to Strike Inside America.'"

"What's that supposed to mean?" Ron stopped short. His suddenly skeptical tone struck me as somewhat impolite, and I grew concerned that he might be in on Amber's plot. Could he be the ringleader, I asked myself?

"It means, 'Don't ignore blatant warnings that are right there in front of your face!'" I think I might have become a little more intense than I'd intended at the end of my warning. I hoped Ron hadn't noticed.

"I think you're overreacting," he said gently, "reading too much into things. You've always been a good neighbor, Jeff, but you need to let this one go." At that moment, I knew he was covering up for what I came to call the Conspiracy.

"Fuck you!" I said. "You're in on it, whatever it is!"

"Get out," Ron demanded. I was offended. Despite his clearly being in the wrong, he continued looking at me crossly, not even listening to my attempts to smooth the situation as he escorted me to his front door.

"You're making a big mistake!" I said as he closed the door.

My plans accelerated at that point, and I needed to call in sick from work. I even had to pretend to be sick so my wife would stop questioning and complaining. I started to think I might have to find a new wife if she didn't become more supportive. At the same time, we had a son together, so I would try to make it work . . . for then.

The bug yielded nothing but plain pleasantries, dull drudgery, and banal bickering. (Evidently Amber and Chad are divorced, unless she caught wind of my listening hole and created a fake recording of family life.) I decided to take action that night. No cultists were going to threaten my son's neighborhood.

At about two in the morning on the fifteenth, my wife and son were asleep. I crept out of our house easily. Getting into Amber's would be the hard part. I had lain our large ladder alongside the house, telling my wife I'd be looking into the rain gutters soon, so I didn't have to raise the garage door to get it out, making a lot of noise, at two in the morning. I carried the ladder the thirty feet across the yard between our houses, set it against Amber's house, and climbed to her roof.

I wasn't sure if I should try to cut a hole in the roof to gain access to her attic or go directly to her bedroom window. Since that was in the back of the house, I decided to go directly. No neighbors would see me; a tree blocked the view to the houses on the next street. And it was two in the morning—no one would be looking for a pudgy guy on a ladder in the middle of the night. Everyone was asleep, or doing better things with his or her time.

I climbed back down the ladder and moved it around her house to the back yard, which required opening her gate. I did so noiselessly, though hefting the ladder through the gate around the corner at night was challenging. The moonlight and cold weather added to my agitation. In my big brown winter coat, I probably looked like a puffed-up tick.

I placed the ladder against the wall just next to the master bedroom window. If all went well, her children would be in their rooms, and it would be Amber and me. I would confront her about her heinous crimes, force her to confess her evil plans toward my son. I would drag her to the police, from whose station I would call Ron, the head of the Homeowners' Association, to gloat.

The window was hard to open, and locked. I decided to abandon secrecy and began pounding on the window to break it. Amber woke and started screaming, then called the police. "Stop right there!" I yelled. "I know what you're doing!" She ran out of the bedroom.

I decided to go around to the front door to confront her from the other direction. I rang the doorbell and pounded on the door itself, bellowing. The housing development began to wake up. "Jeff?" I soon heard from my wife at the front door of our house. "What are you doing?"

"Showing you the truth!" I called back. "Amber, open this door!" She didn't, hiding as usual.

Soon the police arrived, and a crowd of neighbors watched them arrest me. My wife was in tears. My son didn't understand what was happening. But someday he will. His daddy was a hero—after that night, everything has been calm and peaceful in the housing development. I am "under observation" in a medical facility, but this is a pretense, to perpetuate the Conspiracy. I plan to escape soon. My counselor, Gerald, has put on a perfect show of feigned ignorance and fascination.

The only question is which one of us will crack first.

Introduction "A Perfect World"

In October of 2009, I wondered, "We hear all the time that it's not a perfect world. What would a perfect world look like?" First of all, I decided, perfection would look different to every different person. That led me to begin the following exploration of the idea, starring my daughter, Claire, as I envisioned her in high school.

On December 14 and 23, 2011, I polished and extended the story.

"A Perfect World"

Claire opened a door and stepped into a perfect world. She did not know it was perfect at first, except that it seemed completely foreign. Everything was white—the Sky and the Ground, except that the Ground seemed one shade darker than white, an off-white. She saw balls larger than she was slowly rolling about on the Ground, stopping next to one another as if to interact, and moving on occasionally. Claire was confused and intrigued. She closed the door to her world behind her, the door that had, until that moment, been nothing more than the door to the closet in her bedroom.

Approaching a large white ball, Claire could not see anything inside it, though the surface was semi-opaque. The ball seemed to be made of white wax, or layered glass, smoky. Something was inside, she was sure of it.

Claire looked down at her hands, and they too seemed to look different in the light of the strange new place she had found. Suddenly, her hands faded from view, then so did the rest of her! She found herself unable to see any part of herself or her clothing, though she could still think and feel. She tried to walk, and found herself moving in the direction she wanted without feeling herself walking. "This is wonderful!" she thought, and may even have said aloud.

"Isn't it, though?" asked a boy's voice. Claire wanted to see him, and then she did! A very handsome boy of about her age appeared, standing near her, well dressed. "Everything is wonderful here." She had already noticed herself feeling an unusual contentedness.

"Yes, it is!" she agreed. "I have only just arrived here, only I don't know where 'here' is." She looked around, though she still could not see herself. For that matter, she suddenly realized she could no longer see the giant white balls. Now she could only see this boy, and little else. "Who are you? What is this place?" Claire asked.

"This is Perfect World," the boy said. "I'm Nicholas."

"'Perfect World'? What is that?"

"It's where everything is perfect. I'm perfect. You're perfect."

"But what's perfect is different for everybody," Claire protested.

"Exactly," Nicholas said. "I don't really look the way you're seeing me. Your bubble has created the image of me you would find most appealing. If that changes, the image will change."

"I don't believe it. Or understand it. Why would I want your image to change? I wouldn't."

"Oh, you never know," Nicholas said.

"And you're standing right here in front of me," Claire finished.

"Technically, I'm not. You're seeing an image, as I said."

An image? But he seemed as real as anyone standing in front of her ever had. If he wasn't really there, where was he?

"Where are you? Where am I, for that matter? I can't see myself at all."

"I'm in my bubble, seeing the image of you my bubble has created for me. And you are beautiful!

You're in your bubble, seeing an image of me. But you cannot see yourself because your consciousness has been freed of its body. For as long as you remain in your bubble, you will be formless, weightless, and completely comfortable, floating in serenity, surrounded by pleasant images, sounds, and experiences. The entire Universe will be filtered through the bubble for your convenience, in only ways that are pleasing to you."

"Do you mean that if somebody said something mean to me, I would hear it as something kind?"

"You just wouldn't hear anything. If someone doesn't have anything nice to say, he or she doesn't say anything at all."

"Amazing. And a little scary," Claire mused.

"Not at all. It's wonderful, preserves all relationships, and ensures happy cooperation."

"I'd still sort of like the option of telling you to go shit in your hat."

"And because that statement is pleasant to me, I heard it. But I would not if you meant it."

"I see."

"So we can still have a wide-ranging conversation."

"Well, that's good. So, all conversations are respectful?"

"They are."

"Amazing, I say again."

"I don't disagree. It's the way things should be."

"How do you know all this, anyway?"

"A perfect world explains itself. Think of a question, and get a clear explanation."

Claire wondered how such a world could possibly exist. "Accident," she suddenly realized and said.

"That's right," Nicholas answered. "Evolution evolved it into place. These bubbles are like second skins to us all here."

"But how did I get one?" Claire demanded. "I'm not from here. I just arrived! I just stepped in through a door and got a second skin!"

"Perfect, isn't it?" Nicholas laughed. His logic was inescapable.

"Yes, it is."

"There is something about the bubbles that enables them to reach beyond their individual hosts. Evidently they teamed up to create you a bubble, as they seem to have created other bubbles in the past for other visitors and newcomers. You know, we all affect each other."

"So you gave me some skin, in effect?"

"Yes, along with everyone else here."

"How many are there?"

"Oh, I don't know."

"Twenty billion so far, from all over the Galaxy," Claire suddenly said. "Each galaxy has its own perfect world. Amazing."

"Well, there you go," Nicholas said. "Everything is wonderful here, at least until the bubbles run out. But somehow I suspect a perfect world will never allow that to happen."

Claire thought about exploring further. "I want to see some more of this place," she said.

"Certainly. Would you like company, or not?"

"I don't know. I suppose you can't say or do anything unpleasant, so I should theoretically enjoy your company."

"Theoretically. But you never know—I might do something unpleasant just to delight you with the surprise." He smiled at her.

"You can't delight me with something unpleasant." She smiled back. "I wouldn't even know about it, remember? In fact, it wouldn't be unpleasant, because I would know about it if I were being delighted."

"You never know," Nicholas said.

"You're just trying to trick me," Claire said.

2

Claire decided she wanted to walk about and see more, meet more of the persons in that strange place, and told Nicholas so. "Well, you can't walk about, technically. Just will yourself to move in a direction and you will." He smiled.

"Where is my body?" Claire asked.

"Being worked on, regenerated, in your bubble." Nicholas indicated the opaque circle around them, causing Claire to remember with a start that the arm with which he indicated it was an illusion, an "image", too. She had already forgot he didn't look as he appeared to her, and that she was interacting with another disembodied consciousness in the next bubble. The whole thing began to feel slightly creepy to her, so she asked:

"May I leave my bubble again now?"

"Of course."

Claire felt herself becoming more solid, and was particularly struck by the sensation of some unpleasantly heavy things right in the front of her face, until she realized they were her teeth! Soon she was holding up a hand, studying and turning it, marveling at how she felt physically: better than ever! "I'm no longer floating, but I feel the best I've ever felt in my body!" she said.

"Of course," Nicholas said again. "This is a perfect world, in which you improve with age. The bubbles act as literal 'body shops'. The longer you stay in one, the healthier and stronger you'll be."

Claire was stunned. "One could stay here forever."

"Indeed. And we have some citizens who are very old."

Claire wondered what "very old" meant, but didn't yet dare ask. Looking at Nicholas' bubble, she no longer saw his image but a large white bubble like all the rest, indistinguishable. "How will I know which is you?"

"In a perfect world, a way exists," said Nicholas, and his bubble turned orange. "Is that sufficient?"

"Oh, yes!" Claire said. "I like the color orange."

"Then you shall be able to spot me wherever you go. It's a small world."

It's a small world with . . . twenty billion inhabitants, remembered Claire. She began exploring again, with a new eye. Now she understood that each of the big white balls was a person! Perhaps when the balls met they were having a conversation. She would join the nearest one, if they would have her.

She walked over to a threesome of spheres, like every other taller than she. She was not in a bubble ball of her own, so she saw and heard nothing but opaque orbs. "What if I want my bubble back?" she asked herself, and as soon as she did so it began to reappear. She wondered if it came as an extension of the three nearest to her, afraid it would drain their occupants.

"Welcome," she heard almost at the same moment that she felt her body dissolve away again. She saw the images of two men and a woman, all three middle aged, sitting and talking on benches before her.

"Why, thank you!" she said. "I'm Claire."

"Hello, Claire," the three chimed in unison. "Welcome." One of the men motioned for Claire to sit with them, so she willed to do so. Then she found herself seeing them as if from the next seat on the bench, which she knew wasn't there.

"What were you discussing?" Claire asked.

The man who had motioned to her, with black hair, said, "Well, we were discussing how beautiful and perfect everything is, of course, and that we were thinking of dining together this evening."

"You eat here?"

"Oh, yes, of course!" the other man, more portly, said. "But only if you want to. And usually you want to, because the food is always . . . "

"Perfect?" Claire asked smiling.

"Perfect," the man sighed with satisfaction. Claire could tell he liked food.

"May I join you?" Claire asked. "That is, if I'd be welcome, of course."

"Of course!" all three said. "We'd love to have you, dear."

"This isn't at all like Earth," Claire said. "My home."

"Well, of course it is!" said the portly man. "It's just the way Earth should be, and sometimes is." That made Claire think.

"Where are you from?" she asked him.

"Toulouse," he said, suddenly holding and biting into an apple.

"Toulouse!" Claire blurted. "How did you come to live here?"

"I walked into my attic one day," the man said, gesturing widely. "But it had changed." The other two adults laughed. "I've been here since. In a perfect world, my wife doesn't even miss me." He winked.

"You don't mean to tell me there is no way back from here!" Claire worried.

"Not at all, dear child," the woman soothed. "You may go back any time you like. All you need do is imagine the door through which you entered." That thought comforted Claire.

3

At that moment, she noticed her environment changing. The Sky became pink and orange, with a silver sunset over a tranquil blue sea before her, water gently lapping against a white sand beach to her left and right, circling around a large bay that stretched off to the horizon. Behind her, the pink-lit dunes with sparse green grasses sloping upward toward a darkening red sky. "This is beautiful!" Claire cried.

"Your bubble sensed what you needed," the older woman said gently, "before you knew it yourself."

"I could stay here forever," Claire said. "It's beautiful."

"And you would be welcome to do so," said the portly man. "No aging, no disease, no need or want. You don't even need to exercise your body, though you may be as active as you like—with no danger. If you want to jump off a cliff, you can."

"A virtual cliff," corrected Claire.

"True—a virtual cliff. But the experience is the same," the man said. "You get all the thrill with no danger."

"Then where's the thrill?" asked Claire.

"Try it," the man chuckled. Claire decided that could wait until later.

"I think I'll go home now," Claire said.

"You may do that at any time, dear," said the taller, dark-haired man. "Look, there's your door." And so it was: Claire's closet door, at a short distance away from them.

"Thank you," Claire said, surprised again at the speed of the granting of wishes in that place.

"Not at all," the three adults said in different ways as Claire approached the door. She tried to reach out for its doorknob, but didn't see her hand or arm yet. The door opened, and she willed herself to step through.

And she found herself on the other side of the doorway, in her room, holding the doorknob. She turned to find only her closet, filled with clothes, old toys and games, and books, as before.

"Wow," she said aloud. Seeing it was about three o'clock in the morning, she went back to sleep, thinking of her experiences in a perfect world. *When can I go back?* she wondered, then drifted off into blissful, peaceful slumber.

The next day, Claire went through her day at school with perfect calm. She felt she had experienced something that very few human beings had. It was possible that some of her friends had been to the Perfect World, but they would never have told her. She certainly felt she couldn't tell anyone, so how could they have told her? The more that she thought about this problem, the more she felt annoyed, even anguished. A part of her wanted to share her experience with someone else in the Imperfect World—anyone—, but another part of her felt that doing so would lead to charges of insanity and psychological treatment, especially if she insisted it was true. She kept her mouth shut.

Claire's best friend, Emily, was tall, blonde, and athletic, and had recently injured her knee—twice—playing soccer, so was on crutches for the foreseeable future, at least two weeks. Fortunately Emily also worked on the school newspaper, so she could write during long hours spent recuperating. One day she asked Claire if she would like to contribute to the newspaper.

"I would like to write a column called 'A Perfect World', in which I could explore what a perfect world would be like," Claire said. "I could contrast what was happening in the news or at school with how it would happen in that perfect world." Claire felt that was a perfect way of broaching the topic of perfection without sounding crazy.

"I like it," Emily said. "Give me a draft by the end of the week, and we'll work on it for next week's deadline."

Claire was thrilled. She did as Emily asked. Shortly after Emily proofread it, she had a column published in her high school's newspaper. It began thus:

A PERFECT WORLD

In a perfect world, everyone is happy and gets along all the time, including my cats. In the imperfect world we all experience now, cats meow at inconvenient times, play roughly, need to be fed and otherwise cared for (think litter boxes), and even cause many of us terrible allergic reactions. In a perfect world none of this would be a problem. Wouldn't you like that? Imagine a cat who knows when to meow, who does not wake your loved ones or you, who plays sweetly (with no claws out), and who takes care of everything. Could there be any downside of living in a perfect world?

What would a perfect world look like to you?

The next day, she lay on her bed again, wondering when she could visit the Perfect World again. She got up and looked in her closet again but saw only clothes. "This should be a wardrobe," she thought and lay back down. Moments later, she found herself floating up through the ceiling into a world of light and knew she was on her way! Would she see Nicholas again? she wondered.

"I'm here," he said when she arrived, in his orange bubble.

"I'm happy to see you!" said Claire.

"I'm happy to see you too!"

"What shall we do today?" she asked.

"Whatever you like," Nicholas said. "Would you like to ride in a boat on a river?"

"That sounds like fun!" So they did. They spent what felt like hours rowing, relaxing, looking in the water, and talking. They never got hungry or tired. The Sun was not too hot; it was just right. No bugs bothered them. Everything was perfect.

After a while, Claire said she should go home to supper, to be with her family. Nicholas said, "I hope I can see you again soon."

"I'm sure you will," said Claire, very happy.

He gave her a kiss on the cheek, and she was delighted. She left the Perfect World aglow, eager to see Nicholas again soon.

At supper that night, Claire couldn't stop smiling. Her parents asked her why. "Because my life is perfect!" she said. They were surprised.

"Well, that's sweet, Honey," her mother said, before her parents exchanged looks.

The next time Claire saw Nicholas, she said, "You know, everything here is perfect. Being with you is perfect. But knowing that everything here is going to be perfect . . . is kind of boring, don't you think?"

"What do you mean, Claire?" he asked. They were enjoying a perfect picnic on a perfect hillside, with no ants or mosquitos bothering them.

"I mean that everything here is perfect, but it's boring! There's no excitement! Everything is . . . safe. I know there's no danger. It's all controlled."

"I understand what you mean. Yes, that is true. But it's a dangerous world out there, and it's a marvelous world here." He handed her a ball of rainbow-colored light. It was truly amazing.

"That is truly amazing," Claire said, "But a part of the thrill of Life is in not knowing what will happen. Here, all I know is that whatever I imagine will happen, and whatever anyone else says or does will come across as pleasant to me. There's no challenge. I don't even want to jump off a cliff if I know I can't get hurt. I know that sounds strange, but it's true. It's just not *real*. I've enjoyed our times together, but I think—no, I know—I would enjoy them more if they happened in the imperfect world, where anything can happen."

Nicholas' brow grew troubled. "I'm sorry you feel that way, Claire. I have enjoyed our visits too. But I cannot visit with you in the imperfect world. In the imperfect world, I do not look the way I look to you now."

"This is just another example of how everything here is a lie," Claire condemned. "I don't care how you look. I would prefer to see what my friends really look like, and to show them I don't care how they look. I don't care how you look, Nicholas—you are my friend." Nicholas smiled.

"That is sweet, Claire," Nicholas said, "But it is more than the way I look to you, or the way you look to me. I come from a different world. I cannot survive on your planet."

Claire hadn't considered this. "Oh," she said.

"I cannot breathe your atmosphere or tolerate your sun's rays," Nicholas said. "And you could not survive on my planet either. This is the only place we can see each other."

"Oh," she said again.

"I'm sorry," Nicholas said.

"No, I'm sorry," Claire said. "You are my friend, and I do want to stay friends with you. So this is where I'll see you. Deal?"

"Deal."

And that is where they saw each other, from then on. But Claire did not visit the Perfect World too much. She liked the imperfect one more. Reality was the most exciting experience of all, despite its imperfections. The Perfect World might be a fun place to visit, but she wouldn't want to live there.

Claire wanted to live in a place where she could be thrilled by the prospect of not knowing where she would go, what she would do, or what friends she might meet.

And so she did.

Claire had wanted Nicholas to leave the Perfect World in favor of the imperfect world, so they could have exciting adventures together. Now, she knew, that would never be. That was all right, she finally decided, after some time spent in shock and sadness. She was happy they had met, and someday she would ask Nicholas to show her how he looked on his own planet. It occurred to her to wonder what he saw when he looked at her image in his bubble.

Someday, Claire would return to the Perfect World and find out.

Introduction "The Deity" (Unfinished)

In May of 2011, absolutely sick to death of religious claims of a loving deity, I decided to write a story of what, to me, an actual loving deity would look like. Of course, to have a conflict and a plot, I realized that the perfection described in the beginning would have to come to an end. My deity would have to die. The story remains unfinished because once it depicted a normal situation, I lost interest in it. I include it here as I do consider it an interesting idea.

On May 17, when I shared it with a friend, I said, "I hope I continue this story, as I like it. They go through all the usual crap, eventually realizing their own glory. The Deity was good and all, but they like the vigorous life better now."

I left the sex of the narrator ambiguous on purpose.

On October 11, 2012, I added the last three paragraphs.

"The Deity" (Unfinished)

The new day began, as ever before, in the Glory of the Divinity. I had marveled, through the night, as ever before, at the Glory of the Divinity revealed in the Stars. Then I resumed marveling in the day. I sat, I stood, I walked; all was the same. Everyone else did the same. We enjoyed everything and everyone, each other. I saw my friends and they saw me, and we smiled. The golden sunlight bathed us all.

The Deity loved us, and we loved It. There was no other reality. We felt contentment. The days and years passed without change.

Then came the Change. The Deity said to us all, as It had always spoken to us before, in our minds: "Beloved children, we are all as old as Time. But the energy of your deity is not limitless. Your deity is dying. Soon you will be alone. I know you do not understand me, but you will. You must remember that I love you, and I am sorry for leaving you."

We did not understand. We marveled anew. What could it mean? What was "dying"? We knew energy from our world—when we watched the Sun, when we watched a waterfall, we saw energy. But what was death? We could not comprehend this puzzle, our first puzzle. All had been known and understood before.

What was "alone"? What was "leaving"? We knew not the meanings of these new words. We lived as before.

One day, we felt a great emptiness. Some began to say that the Deity had died, had left us. We could feel it, most of us, though some still held out hope. We did not know what it was we felt; we had never felt any suffering, so we had no words to describe what we felt. I felt new sensations and emotions coursing through my body, which felt different in its entirety somehow. I no longer felt contentment only. Something changed.

Everything looked the same, but everyone felt differently. The Great Harmony that had existed until then had ceased. The majority, myself included, continued to rely on the Deity, though it was silent. Where had it gone? We did not even have the words to ask that question at the time, though we felt the lack. We felt the greatest emptiness inside. Some faces became ugly and distorted. Some said, "We are going. We know not where. We will not return." We knew not why they did this. I felt a sensation in my breast I had not felt before, a great pain. I have the word now. It has been created. We have created, in the Deity's absence.

The planet changed. The air became cold, and wet. We became cold. We went indoors, but this was not sufficient. We had to place materials onto our bodies to protect us. We could not understand why this was happening. Why did our deity leave us? Why did our deity die? Why was that the order of things? Why had our deity not prepared us better? We were happy, and I wanted nothing more than to return to our ageless happiness without suffering.

We noticed a change in ourselves. We became ugly and weak, then ceased to function. This was the greatest horror. Our deity was punishing us, it seemed. What had we done? Where did our loved ones go when they ceased? We assumed they followed the Deity, who had said it was "dying". We called this new change in our people "the Dying". The Dying continues to this day, though we hope for its cessation with the return of our deity.

I am Cordra. I was a leader of our people. We had no need of leaders before. Then, we struggled for resources. We required food, which we had not required before. We had to cease our activity at night. Our bodies were weak and frail. We gained strength at times, but our energy was limited. It is the Hateful Condition, and it continues to this day. We realized that, in the absence of replenishment, our number was dwindling. We had to find a way to survive before we all died.

Another aspect of the Change was that we found ourselves drawn to each other in a way that produces a loss of mind. I found myself unable to think or feel clearly when I saw or spoke with Arden. I could not understand this; Arden and I had passed innumerable days and years in quiet contemplation and conversation on the wonders of the Deity, the Universe, and the Stars. Why should I then be experiencing difficulty when faced with this old friend?

Arden, too, expressed the same. I felt strange sensations and emotions. I could not understand what was happening. Something had transformed us. I did not feel the same calm equanimity I had known before, the only state I had ever known. We came to pass all our time together. We wanted nothing more than to be together. We did not know why. We enjoyed our time together. We attributed these things to the will of the Deity.

The cold, the heat, the changes of the air and ground confounded us all. Some ceased due to these changes. The rest of us made changes to continue.

We learned. We grew. These were things we had not done before.

Arden and I did things we could not explain or understand. We found ourselves creating a new person, as if we were the Deity!

Our existence had been formless and timeless. We went from floating in white space, consciousnesses touching and mingling without shape, to subsisting in weighted form, trapped by our skins, subject to every shock we now suffer. We now have an end, we know not when. The distance we feel from each other, even if we sit next to each other, cannot be expressed. The sorrow is barely endurable.

Some did and do not endure it. They took and take their own lives in despair. We did not even know the significance of dying when it began. Now, we do. We have learned much through heavy pain and suffering . . . much we had no need of knowing before. We did not even have words for these things, but now we do. We have gained many words through our sad trial.

Some questioned how our deity could do this to us. Those of us who remained loyal answered, "Our deity did not do this to us. Our deity would not do this to us by choice. Our deity is ended, like the others. Our deity warned us, but we had no way to understand what the warning meant. If we can fault our deity for anything, it is for not preparing us. Perhaps our deity did not expect to die. If so, our deity made a mistake and is at fault for that mistake, but this is of no import. Regardless of the cause,

Our deity
~~who~~ could not,
prevent it, and
to complain you must remember that I love you
was pointless Deity had said. and I am sorry for leaving you,

nothing can be done. Now we are alone, and what was
becomes of us is our choice. Our loss is both a curse enough
and a blessing, in that we are now the masters of our for
fates." ← for me.

We came to learn how to live
while suffering. We came to learn
how not to talk about our
suffering, despite our shock,
because we learned that doing
so added to the burden of
the others. Then we learned
~~to care~~ that the others
cared regardless, as we did—
our own burdens did not
stop us from caring for
the burdens of ~~others~~

We discovered others, not
just children of the Deity
such as we were. We
found other forms, what

Introduction "Mister Negative"

"Do you criticize your friends, or do you keep your thoughts to yourself? Which do you consider to be true friendship? If a friend of yours did something you felt was foolish, would you say so? If so, how would you phrase it?" This is what I asked some friends on April 15, 2012, after another friend made some statements to me that I considered quite foolish. I wanted to tell her so, but I did not dare, for fear of causing offense.

That friend herself, perhaps sensing my questions were about her, said, "Context is crucial. If you're a friend, you will be aware of whatever their struggles are at that time, and choose to refrain from dumping more on them. I'm sure you'll say that is dishonest and you can't bear it. Context is crucial across the board. Some people simply are not looking for criticism. That is their own thing, and respecting their boundaries at that time is vital. If your friend has expressed a desire for such openness and unrestrained honesty, then by all means knock yourself out."

In other words, "Back off. I'm not interested in being criticized by you about this right now." Okay, fine. However, once again tired of being misunderstood ("I'm sure you'll say that is dishonest and you can't bear it"), I did my best to enlighten her:

> On the contrary, I am constantly refraining from saying what I think to be diplomatic, though even Robin [my

wife] doesn't believe me, which is why I said yesterday, 'This world doesn't know what honesty/criticism/negativity is. I'm going to write a story about a character named Mister Negative and let the World behold true negativity!'

Robin asked, 'Why would anyone read it?'

I don't know, but it struck me as a good way to blow off the steam that I'm never blowing.

That was the truth, but after thinking of the story on the fourteenth, I sketched some notes that did not satisfy me, erased them, and gave up on the idea, except in a distant, "That would be a good idea someday," kind of way.

One of my friends, Keanu Allridge, responded, "I'd read it, Robert!"

That gave me the encouragement I needed. I immediately wrote what became my second story written in one sitting. I wanted it to be as negative as could be, but I also wanted it to be amusing. Over the next several weeks, delighted by the premise and plot, I added vignettes and details, though the gist remained the same. The story grew and grew.

One of the anecdotes I added after the first draft was that of the Bistro West. This unfortunate dining experience did occur as described, though I did not respond as vigorously to it as Mister Negative did. For the record, every detail of that experience is true. My wife, Robin, and I ate there in Los Angeles in December 2001. Two months (not the two weeks in the story) after our worst dining experience, we saw that the place had closed, most deservedly so. Also, the remarks I attribute to Plus after the couple returns home are verbatim quotations from my wife regarding the experience.

Please note this character is *not me*. The whole point of this story is to say, "You think I'm negative? Here's negative."

My wife's position now is simply that though it is possible to be even more negative than I am, I am still too negative for her. I am sorry, Honey, and I will try to work on that. At least I got a story out of my negativity exaggerated . . . a story my wife hates and could not bear to read.

Different persons like different things. Keanu's position, and hopefully that of anyone who might like this story, is, "Neg's meanness is what gives the story its mean charm!" That was certainly my intent.

I will add that writing this story *was* a good way to blow off steam. I felt a great catharsis upon finishing my first draft, because it felt very good to let out thoughts and feelings I had never fully discharged in my up-to-then-lifelong effort to be "positive", whatever that means. I sometimes think that "positive" means either "Take shit and like it," or, at the very least, "Say you're happy when you're not." What bullshit. How about, "When you're happy, say so, and when you're not happy, say so, because there is nothing wrong with saying how you feel or speaking your mind"? Shocking, I know.

I saw the "complainer" sign on a wall at SUNY Stony Brook over twenty years ago. It has bothered me ever since. What stupidity.

"Mister Negative"

"You're a stupid, fat, ugly, lazy whore!" Mister Minus Negative said into his bathroom mirror, jabbing his finger at his own reflection, then chuckled and checked his teeth before going to work. His wife was downstairs with their children.

"All right, you fucking punks," he said to his children as he came downstairs. "I want you to break a leg today. Don't take any crap, okay?"

"You got it, asshole," said his son, X.

"That's my boy."

"I'll give it," said his daughter, Y.

"Good girl."

The phone rang.

Mister Negative answered it. "Hello? It's a little early for a call."

"Good morning. Please hold for an important message from—"

He hung up.

The phone rang again.

Mister Negative answered it again.

"—Marketicks. We would like to invite you to participate in an important survey. If you answer our five questions, you will receive a free two-day cruise in the Caribbean!"

"Blow me slowly," Mister Negative said and hung up.

He kissed his wife, Plus (née Positive), and two children and walked to his local bus stop, wondering why the world hated honesty and even joking. "Shithead" could be a term of endearment, but this world was having none of that. Because he hated sunshine, he carried an umbrella made of a large piece of black industrial plastic that a friend had made for him; fabric umbrellas did not block enough sun to suit him, and he had to go to work. He could not hide from the Sun at home every day of his life, though he often wished he could.

On his way out the front door, he saw his next-door neighbors, Mister and Mistress Putz, sitting on their front steps with their young son. "Good morning," Mister Putz said.

"It would have been good, except I bumped into you," Mister Negative said. "Why can't you stay in your house at this time of day?"

"Well, excuse me," said Mister Putz.

"No, I will not, you idiot," said Mister Negative. "And another thing, Putz: your dog keeps shitting in my yard, and you keep not picking it up. If you don't cut it out, I'll put it in your mailbox. I might even wait until your convertible top is down. Do you understand me?"

"Affirmative, Negative."

"Good. In the future, please stop talking to me. We live next to each other, that is all. That does not give us anything in common other than the street. I have my own thoughts to think, and seeing me does not give you the right to disturb my tranquility, so shove your 'good mornings' up your ass. Your boy's still got bad teeth, I see."

As he walked away, Mistress Putz said to her husband, "I don't see much tranquility there."

On his way to his local bus stop, Mister Negative saw two young men knocking at a door across the street. They were dressed very professionally, but something about their manner gave Neg pause.

"Excuse me, young men," he called out to them. "Would you like to talk with me?"

Since no one seemed to be answering the door at which they were knocking, they looked at each other. "Sure," one of them said to him. They came across the street to where he was.

"What are you boys doing in our fine neighborhood on this fine day?" Mister Negative asked.

"We're preaching the Word of the Lord," one of them said. "We're saving souls. Do you own a Bible, Sir?"

Mister Negative burst out laughing.

"Sorry, no, boys." He chuckled some more and wiped a tear from one eye. Then he took a long look at their youth and naiveté. "You know what? I'm feeling charitable today, so I'll just say that I wish your souls and you luck. Have a good day."

"You too, Sir," they said.

Mister Negative made it to the bus stop at the end of his block rather quickly. On the side of it was a sign someone had put up, apparently directed at him, reading, "NOBODY LIKES A COMPLAINER."

"Starting with you," he said to the sign. "Complaints are all that lead to progress." He understood the sign meant "whiner". As usual, the World was not clear enough. He ripped it down, crumpled it up, and threw it into the nearby garbage pail. "Idiots," he muttered.

Feeling better, he sat down on the bus-stop bench. A young woman sat there already.

"Ugly dress," he commented on her black-and-white polka-dotted dress.

"Who asked you?" she demanded.

"Oh, fuck off, you stupid cunt," he said. "I'm trying to help you here."

She stopped speaking with him, completely ungrateful for his fashion advice.

Such exchanges with other human beings, which occurred daily, did not disturb Mister Negative; he was used to the misunderstanding of others. In high school, he had been called a "spoil sport". At nineteen, he had been told he had "no sense of humor" and was "depressing to be around". Since he had become an adult, he had been told he was "too negative". He felt that the World didn't know what negative *was*.

"The truth hurts," the World said.

"The lie hurts," he said. "The truth heals." So he decided to put his sharp tongue to use.

That is why he worked in radio.

"Hey, you stupid fuckers," he greeted his colleagues as he walked into the station. They responded with cordial greetings. *At least they get me here*, he thought. *What a bunch of fucking morons outside. Well, that's why I get paid the big bucks to enlighten them, right?* He chuckled at that thought. The day they paid him big bucks for delivering the unvarnished truth would be the day he'd think he died and went to Heaven—or was dreaming. No, the World (beyond his niche audience) didn't want the Truth.

He opened and closed his show each day with the words, "Mister Negative. Strong as a skunk. Thanks for seeking the spray."

The first caller asked if everything was hopeless.

"No," Minus Negative, or "Neg" as he called himself, said. "Everything is not hopeless. I get out of bed every day. I love to be alive, and I consider myself a very hopeful guy. I just *hope* that everybody else gets a fucking clue. That is a general comment, not directed at you. I mean, look at this fucking rock called the Planet Earth: we've got billions dying, fighting, starving, torturing each other, and slaving away to pursue fantasies of wealth or beauty that will never come true. Meanwhile, the real overlords of this planet continue to destroy it *and you* with pollution and claim it's all natural. By the way, buy some more crap you don't need to put into your house you can't afford while you take an expensive vacation burning more fossil fuels that will destroy the planet for your children. I don't know about you, but I'm fucking pissed! I have two children, and you're telling me that I'm negative? Fuck you!"

"It's really them that are negative, because they want to negate the truth," the caller said.

"Thank you!" Neg said. "They want to negate my concerns and statements, yes, they do. They just want me to shut up and go away. Not going to happen. In fact, why don't you bite my big, fat hairy wet one, World? Next caller."

"I think you're a disgusting, immoral dreg of Humanity," the next caller said.

"Well, fuck you too," Neg said.

"There is so much beauty in this world," the caller said, "and all you do is focus on the negative."

"Listen: I'm supposed to be happy about a world where we spend our lives slaving away for assholes who take all the profits and ass-rape us without lube? I would suggest to you you're living in a fantasy land if you think the current societal arrangement is in any way desirable for anyone except those who sit on our backs riding us like mules. You are, in fact, an idiot. You aid and abet slavery and ignorance with your own mental slavery and sel-imposed ignorance. Go to Hell. Rather, stay there!" Neg hung up on that one. "Next caller."

After a hard day of truth, Neg went home, feeling refreshed. It exhilarated him to get his candid thoughts out of his system. He carried no burden, felt no pressure from stifling his thoughts. He got them out and moved on.

On the bus ride home, Neg saw a sign on the inside of the bus that read, "Resentment hurts you not them."

"I resent this sign," he chuckled.

He caught a nun staring at him. She said, "Young man, it is obvious to me that your soul is in trouble."

"Penguin," he said, "the only thing troubling my soul is bullshit like yours." She went back to her own thoughts. "What's black and white and red all over?" he called out to her, taunting her without expecting or receiving a response.

After Neg got off the bus, as he was walking toward his home, he saw a truck about to hit a boy on a bicycle. He shouted, "Hey!" and ran as fast as he could toward the boy, reaching him just in time to push him out of the way of the truck, which then hit him. "Ahh!" he shouted as he was thrown to the pavement. He began to moan in pain. The driver of the truck got out, saying, "I'm so sorry! I didn't see the boy! Are you okay?"

"What does it look like, you fucking moron! Call a fucking ambulance, will you? Are you all right?" Neg looked over to the boy, who nodded. "Good. Now go home and play, because there is nothing better on this world that you can do." The boy hesitated. "Go. Enjoy yourself. That's what it's all about." The boy looked at the other man, who nodded, then started peddling home.

The driver of the truck said, "I think the quickest way to get you help would be to drive you to the hospital myself." Neg agreed to let him.

They arrived at the emergency room. Neg called his wife to let her know what was going on, but he urged her to stay at home. He said he was fine, and that the kids needed to stick to their routine. She honored his wish.

Neg learned he had a broken leg. This he knew. After setting it and placing it in a cast, the staff asked him if he had a ride home, and he said no. The driver of the truck offered to drive him home again. "It's the least I can do, I feel so bad." So Neg let him, and the drive home was uneventful.

"People are fucking morons," Neg said the next day. "And this driver wasn't even a moron. He had an accident—these things happen. That's not what I'm talking about. I'm talking about the people who don't think about the consequences of their actions or beliefs. You feed the poor but pursue policies that perpetuate poverty? That makes you an idiot, a hypocrite, or both. Ah, it's disgusting. This whole planet is disgusting. I'm depressed, my friends."

His first call that morning was from the Mayor.

"Mister Negative, I heard about what happened to you yesterday," the Mayor said, "and I want to express my personal sorrow over it. Someone who suffers as much as you do needs not to suffer any more."

"Is this some trick?" Neg asked his staff to verify the call.

"Not at all. I know how much the slings and arrows of outrageous fortune and total lunacy frustrate you—if anything, you are the most caring citizen in this town, working night and day to enlighten us, and your gifts are rarely appreciated for what they are."

"I am shocked!" Neg said. "This can't be true."
"But it is," the Mayor said. "But that's not why I'm calling. I'm calling because I heard what happened yesterday: you saved a boy from being hit by a truck, and I want to thank you by giving you the Key to the City tomorrow at City Hall. That is, if your injury will allow it."

"Well!" said Neg. "I think I can manage to limp down there."

"Excellent. We'll see you there."

"Thank you, Mister Mayor. Now, could you do something about our garbage pickup?"

The next day, Neg played a previously recorded show to cover his shift while he went to City Hall for a visit with the Mayor. The Mayor stood with him, gave him the Key to the City, and posed for photographs with Mister Negative.

"Mister Negative, you are our greatest citizen, because you, like Socrates and others before you, are the fly buzzing at the horse's ass of Society. You prick our conscience. You point out the flaws in our thinking. You make us think. For us not to honor you would be a great ingratitude for all you do to make our lives better."

"Is that an endorsement to succeed you?" Neg asked. The Mayor laughed.

Some, however, were less than amused. "Down with negativity!" one man called out from the crowd.

"Hey, fuck you!" Neg shouted as the television cameras rolled. The Mayor chuckled nervously. "If I didn't have this broken leg, I'd teach you some fucking manners!" Neg threatened.

"You don't know shit about manners!" the man in the crowd yelled back.

"Now, now, ladies and gentlemen—and Neg," the Mayor said. "I'm sure we can all treat each other cordially today."

"Fuck that shit," Neg said. "I'm out of here." He started to use his crutches to leave. "You're all a bunch of pieces of shit, as far as I'm concerned. Except you, Mister Mayor. You're too nice."

Plus drove them home.

"Well, that was nice, dear," she said on the drive home. "It was very nice of the Mayor to give you the Key to the City."

"Yes, yes, it was," Neg said. "I had a good time, until that asshole opened his mouth."

"Not everyone is as considerate as you, dear."

"That's for sure."

"But there is something you might consider, the next time you call someone a name or berate him for not being as brilliant as you are."

"Oh? What's that?"

"You can say what you think without being mean about it. There is such a thing as tact. I don't always agree with you, but at least I'm polite about it, because I love you."

"And I love you," he said, "but sometimes even being unkind is necessary to provoke thought and, therefore, change.   I am unkind to racism, for example.   Racists are evil bastards.   The tobacco industry, for another example, is a bunch of drug pushers who should be in jail under current law, but the FDA's a bunch of fucking cowards. I've said it for years, and I'll say it again: the whole World is crazy. And stupid."

"Just something to consider."

"Okay. Now consider this question: when did being 'nice' become our highest goal, and why? Someone who steals office, steals the Treasury, depresses the Economy, and starts unprovoked wars while lying about them is an evil man, and there is not only nothing wrong with saying so, it is our obligation to do so, so we can teach our children the difference between right and wrong, and so we never again make the mistake of trusting such a villain. I sometimes think that those who advocate gentility do so because they are the chief beneficiaries of it; in other words, they themselves do not wish to be exposed in their own evil."

"I'm not evil. I'm just kind, and that is a part of being kind."

"I don't wish to be kind to everyone. I'm sorry. I think the most kindness some deserve is death, but because I'm not allowed to euthanize them, all I can do is point out their worthlessness and negative effect on Humanity."

"Don't you think your effect on Humanity is negative?"

"No, my effect on *them* is negative—not on Humanity itself. I'm the garbage man. It's my job to find the trash, which is very carefully disguised on this world. Telling the truth is just another public service."

"Not everyone wants or appreciates the service."

"That's for sure. Well, we don't always know what's good for us."

"And I'm tired of losing friends when you embarrass me. I'm tired of being in the middle. You either don't respect or even understand the concept of interpersonal boundaries."

"Unless I have been asked to do otherwise, I will offer help where I perceive a need to *all*, not just 'friends'. I call that 'being moral'. But I never force myself on anyone. I say what I think more than most, and I do get in trouble for it. I consider that a reflection on those who cannot handle even slight grains of truth, not on the one providing them. Honesty is the best policy, right?"

"There's honesty, and there's just being rude and obnoxious. You say things that are mean and uncalled for. You violate privacy, telling people things about me against my will. You violate propriety with almost your every utterance."

"Propriety? Fuck propriety!"

"I rest my case. You interrupt me, which I don't do well with; you misunderstand me because you think I mean things that I don't; and you think you've gotten the gist when there is more information to be given, but, because you've interrupted me, I haven't been able to get it all out yet. You're a workout, Neg."

"I think I'm pretty easy."

"Are you fucking kidding me? You make everything hard!"

This was of course something Neg had heard before, though he had never agreed. He considered his response carefully.

"I think the rest of the World makes things hard."

"You always think it's the rest of the World, not you. Never you."

"It is!"

"Of course it is. Well, I can tell you what's best for me. What's best for me is a husband who isn't an asshole!

"I can't take it anymore, Minus," Plus said. "If you don't stop it with me, our family, and our friends—you can say what you want on your show—you're going to end up alone. And that's not a threat; that's just the truth. Is that what you want?"

"No. You're right. I'm sorry," he said at length. He resolved to himself to hold his negative fire in most instances, reserving it for when it was needed most. "I'll be nicer in general, I promise."

"Hallelujah," Plus said. "You come on too strong, Minus. There's a nice way to say things, and there's a dick way to say things. And you always choose the dick way. You're too aggressive. People can't handle someone who says what he thinks the way you do. You're so forceful that they get scared."

"I find that many persons don't like my taking offense . . . from offense. They don't like being held accountable for what they do. They run away screaming, crying, and blaming me for being a big bastard, when all I've done is share my thoughts on their bad behavior. That's the story of my life."

"Hold them accountable, but do it in a more diplomatic way, okay?"

"Okay, my love."

That night, the Negatives decided to dine out to celebrate Neg's new reasonableness. Of course, it must be stipulated (he stipulated it several times) that he was only going to withhold his fire until it was proved that someone else needed it—not that he hadn't felt it necessary before, but henceforth he would impose a higher threshold on his "rules of engagement". He wouldn't issue his form of "help" to every stranger on the street or bus, for example. They decided to visit the Bistro West, a new café that had opened up in town about a month before. A musician friend of theirs, Ali Handal, would also be playing there that night, so it was decided. Neg vowed to behave himself.

When they arrived, Ali was already playing in the corner. They waved, and she smiled. A young woman with platinum blonde hair led the Negatives to their table, the paper on which was covered with water and written on with ink.

"I guess you're busy tonight," Neg joked, making the effort to be kind. The waitress laughed.

The Negatives sat down at the table, expecting someone to come clean up the table, but no one did. Eventually the waitress went by again, and Neg asked, "Excuse me, Miss, but is someone going to clean this?"

"In just a minute," the waitress said. When the waitress came back, she took off the paper and put on new. The table, being still wet, dampened the new paper, but at least it wasn't written on.

The Negatives ordered drinks. Plus ordered wine, Neg ordered iced tea.

"This iced tea tastes like water with sawdust mixed in," Neg said to Plus. "Could I have a Coke instead?" he asked the waitress when they were fortunate enough to see her again.

"Yes, but there'll be a delay while we add carbonation to the Coke."

"Okay," Neg said.

She left again.

The Negatives waited for a while.

"I wonder what's taking them with my wine," Plus said.

"I don't know," Neg said.

When they saw the waitress go by again, Neg asked her about the wine.

"I'll be bringing both drinks together," she answered in an annoyed tone.

"Why?" he asked her.

The waitress pretended not to hear him. Eventually she brought Plus's wine, which she set down on the table along with Neg's Coke, before departing again. Plus took a sip of her red wine.

"This wine is refrigerated," she said in surprise. "This is the first time in my life I have had red wine refrigerated."

"Ask for a different glass," Neg suggested.

"I will. Excuse me, sir?" Plus asked the host/owner, a young man with a cocky attitude, who was the only other staff person walking about serving anyone. He came over to them. "This wine is chilled," Plus told him. "Could I please have a glass that's room temperature?"

"Of course," the man said. He returned a few minutes later with a glass of wine that was much warmer than room temperature. After giving it to Plus with a smile, he moved on to visit another table.

"I can't believe this," Plus whispered to Minus. "This wine has been microwaved. On top of that, it isn't very good wine."

Neg had seen and heard enough.

"Hey, what kind of place are you running here?" Neg demanded of the owner loudly, across a few tables of customers. "You should be ashamed of yourself. You're trying to trick us, but you're inept. Either that, or you really just have no clue about how to run a business. Which is it?"

The owner turned red, looked about himself and laughed nervously, then suddenly remembered something in the kitchen, and walked away.

The Negatives were disgusted, but they were hungry, so they stayed.

After several more minutes, supper arrived. The waitress set down Neg's salad and Plus' ravioli, which Plus recognized. After the waitress left, Plus whispered to Neg, "This pasta is from Costco. I've bought this same pasta there myself. They obviously don't have a chef."

"No tip," Neg said. "Tips are for good service, and this place licks donkey balls."

Plus could not argue with that last assessment.

From delivering the food on, the waitress, now their enemy, ignored the Negatives. But they were hungry, and the portions were so small they were still hungry after they finished them, so they requested bread and olive oil. The waitress brought them with a grunt.

When the Negatives received the bill, they were shocked to see the sum of $38.88. Neg's Cokes were nine dollars (three dollars each!), because the waitress hadn't told them there were no free refills, and there was so much ice in each glass that only about four ounces in each were Coke.

"Wow," Neg said.

"No tip," Plus said.

Neg gave his card. The waitress took it and came back. Neg wrote $38.88 with no tip, and they left.

By the time they were home, eating a necessary second helping of supper, they were laughing about how bad it had been.

"The waitress wasn't even classy enough for a titty bar, she was so trashy," Plus said. "And she smelled bad."

"Honey!" Neg said, delighted.

"Well, it's true!" Plus said. "The waitress was such a bitch. She was so gross!"

Neg was on cloud nine of negativity.

"We spent thirty-eight dollars on dinner and I'm hungry," Plus said.

Neg emailed Ali that night to tell her about their experience: "We think you're great and we loved your performance tonight, but we had to get out of there."

"Wow!" Ali wrote back the next morning. "I'm sooooo sorry about your experience, and I'm glad you told me! Unbelievable. I won't be playing there again—that's just crazy! I also heard from another friend that they tried to overcharge her for dinner and poured her wine to just a half a glass. Yikes!"

"Yikes, indeed," Neg said. "I suppose being positive only goes so far."

That waitress better not give up her day job sucking cocks, Neg thought.

"Come to think of it, only free sexual favors would have redeemed that dining experience," he said on the air the next day. "Then again, with their ineptitude, I'm not sure I'd want to trust them to tasks of that delicacy." He chuckled. "That place again: Bistro West. B-I-S-T-R-O West. Do not go there, or you will be under pain of gastrointestinal tract and wallet. They couldn't even handle a salad."

"You're obnoxious!" said the first caller, Dan in Ohio. "Keep up the good work!"

"Thank you, my friend!" Neg said. "I'm glad you understand what I'm doing. With no training, I could do a better job running that restaurant. Why? Because I'm honest. I wouldn't hide my charges from you. I wouldn't bill you falsely. I also care enough not to leave a table messy or ignore my customers, let alone serve them bullshit food and drink." He sighed. "It's all bullshit.

"It's not that I'm being *mean* to those idiots at that restaurant. It's that I'm honestly describing what they did. And if you don't want the World to think you're a fucking idiot, *don't be a fucking idiot*! It's called *personal responsibility*, which no one seems to understand. Everyone's 'polite', but the truth is that everyone says the same things I do—they just do it behind everybody else's backs. Which do you prefer, open hostility or pretense of approval? I'd rather know where I stood with somebody than worry all the time that he or she was going to knife me in the back. And the reality—another painful reality I am going to acknowledge for you—is that those who mean well cause us more harm than those who do not, which is why Machiavelli said it was better to be feared than loved. Those admirers will fuck you up. Next caller, Kimberly in Washington."

"Hi, Neg. At the risk of fucking you up, I have to agree with Dan. You're just very comfortable with who you are. That allows you to be completely open and honest, a trait that many have had issue with. Being open and honest with yourself is required before you can be that way with others. I have to censor myself with a lot of people, for different reasons."

"Yeah, that stinks," said Neg. "I'm sorry. But I'm glad you know a friend when you hear one. Who tells it to you straight but a friend? I'm the truest friend this town has! Next caller."

A couple weeks later, Plus and Neg happened to pass the Bistro West and saw that it was permanently closed. "Ye reap what ye sow," Neg said to Plus.

"I'd like to read to you an email I got from April in Hawaii," Neg said on the air the next day. "She says: 'It isn't that disagreement is categorically triggering but that you disagree so vehemently, so much, about everything, and it can be interpreted as if other people are all wrong and you alone are right. Sorry to be blunt, just sayin'. Most of us aren't fazed, and we love you for you, but some people just want to feel good for a while during their crappy day and it rubs them wrong. Many people have a lot of stress in their lives, and they don't want more.'

"I understand that, April, and you never need to say you're sorry for being blunt with me. Here's my problem: feeling strongly as I do has been misinterpreted many times, both that 'others are all wrong and I alone am right' and that I am inflexible. Both of these interpretations are shockingly absurd, of course, but I have concluded that most persons simply do not understand the nature of feelings. I think and feel; I share my thoughts and feelings. My opinions, though not my basic views, can turn on a dime, if I am persuaded to change them. And yet, because my opinions are strong when they occur, too much is read into them. Then I am told to tone it down so as not to be misunderstood. Let me ask you this, April: where is Society's obligation not to be stupid?

"I am continually being misunderstood for saying what I think! I cannot be clearer, and yet I get the message from some of you that I am supposed to say less. It's not that you want to understand; it's that you don't want the truth. You just want the truth to go away and never bother you again. You actually *like* jumping to wrong conclusions and thinking wrong things, because it's easier.

"Here's the World's biggest example of this: if we do bad things to our planet, bad things will happen to our planet. Big shock, I know, and yet for some reason, even that logic problem is too hard to solve! We are polluting ourselves out of existence! Where do the oil and gas people think they're going to hide from the consequences of *their actions* while they murder the rest of us? But, I know, the truth is hard work. It's hard to figure out that if you destroy your planet, you won't have a planet to live on! 'I guess we'll all just book a flight on Planet Med!'

"Here's another good example, in an email from Caroline in North Carolina, in response to a recent discussion of untimely death: 'Because of man's rebellion and choice to leave God out of the picture, bad things do happen, but God is in the business of redeeming people and situations. Good can come from terrible situations. In the case of someone dying young, it is a shame for them to have died, but death is the main side effect of the original sin. That's just how it is—it was man's choice. Even so, God does often work things together so that good comes from sad events.'

"You hear that, World? You are being punished for someone else's supposed crime by a god who knew everything in advance and set it in motion anyway. I don't know about you, but I'm tired of such malarkey.

"Look: the truth is, you're going to die. You're going to die. And then you're done. There is no fairy-tale Daddy or Mommy in the Sky. You're going to be worm-meat. And in all likelihood, you deserve nothing better, and the World will be a better place for your absence. Because as I look about me today, on television, on my way to work, and out the window in my building, I see a—what did George Lucas call it? A wretched hive of scum and villainy. That's the human race in a nutshell, and you all stink!

"You say I'm supposed to treat your crazy beliefs—no matter how absurd they are—with 'respect'. What makes you think that? Worst of all, you expect me to act as if I agree with you! That's not respect—that's 'flattery'. Look it up. I believe that Christina Hendricks is my mistress. Are you going to treat that statement with the respect that it deserves, or are you going to flatter me for my approval? Bullshit on that!

"If I say Christina Hendricks created the Universe and life after death, and I know this to be true because a book written by men in the street outside says so, you will laugh in my face and say I'm pulling your leg. Why should it be any different if I change the name 'Christina Hendricks' to 'God', 'Allah', 'Vishnu', or 'Cookie Monster'? I'm pulling your leg either way! To quote Tickle-Me Emo, which I love to do as often as circumstances permit, there is no god. No god!

"Caroline, your loving god says, 'You're on your own, here's some collective punishment for you, and, by the way, it's your fault. If you grovel pretty I'll forgive what I did to you.' I have a much different idea of a loving god, I'll tell you that, but because I do not believe in any god, I don't have to reconcile this miserable world with one. Caroline, to me yours is what Nietzsche called a slave mentality, trying to rationalize the biggest abuser ever imagined. (And yes, the word is 'imagined'.) An acquaintance of mine once pointed out that the Abrahamic religions are essentially BDSM relationships, in which one half of the power exchange is made up. Their adherents love this arrangement, because their fantasy Dom has absolute power over them and their lives. He can reward or punish them, they are helpless, and if they don't worship Him properly He'll whip their asses. I'm not into that, sorry. I have too little control over my own life as it is; I'd much rather just learn to live with things as they are. Evidently religious persons don't want to or can't. I pity them, really. Life is much more interesting and exciting when you realize it's all no more than it appears to be: a beautiful random occurrence.

"And they call *me* negative. They don't know what negative is." Neg sighed. "Next caller. Jane in Oregon."

"Neg, maybe a lot of people find it irritating not that you have opinions that differ from their own but that you act like a bulldozer and run people down if *they* disagree with *you*," the woman said.

"It's really hard to quantify, but I hear this constantly in your show, and you've upset many of your listeners. If you don't like *Firefly*, for example, that's fine! Lots of people don't! And lots of people manage to express that they don't without overtly suggesting that anyone who does like *Firefly* must be a huge fucking idiot. This is just one example. It's an attitude. No one cares if you don't share their opinion! They care if they are going to be treated like they are stupid."

"I am sure they do find it irritating," Neg said. "I agree with you. At the same time, anyone who likes *Firefly* is a huge fucking idiot." He laughed. "No, I have never said that. What I said was that the show is a bad Han Solo ripoff. I don't think those who like it are idiots; I just think they have bad taste. And I'm allowed to say that. Why do we have mouths, if not to say what we think?

"Listen, Jane: I used to keep my thoughts to myself, and all that caused me was pain and suffering. Now I say what I think as much as possible, and, unfortunately, on this perfect planet, there is much to criticize and condemn. My wife told our daughter yesterday that life is, unfortunately, mostly pain and suffering. I don't agree with her about 'mostly', but there certainly is a hell of a lot of it. There is also human folly. And you're telling me I'm not allowed to talk about it? What's it to you? What do you care if I complain that my tongue is ticklish, my teeth itch, or my neighbor can't remember to pick up after his dog?"

"I'm a person who cares about everyone," she said, "and I just think your interactions would go better, and you yourself would be happier, if you tried to be a little more charitable toward everyone. Maybe instead of saying what you think 'as much as possible', you should be more selective."

"I'm very charitable," Neg said. "I'm just tired of making allowances for things that shouldn't even be happening.[1] The worst thing you can say about me is that I'm honest. Based on all that I see in this world, I think I'm doing okay. You have a good day, now, you hear? Thanks for the advice." He ended the call.

"For the record," he continued on the air, "I don't call everyone who disagrees with me a huge fucking idiot. (I actually enjoy being corrected when I am wrong, because I enjoy learning. I never said I was always right.) Those who disagree with me might be right. They might persuade me I am wrong. But those who fail to do so, those who I still feel are wrong, I call wrong. Those who I feel are stupid I call

---

[1] Neg asked me to add, "And if you begrudge me saying things shouldn't be happening, you begrudge me exercising my independent judgement at all. And *I'm* the asshole? No, it's you."

stupid. What—I'm not supposed to call out error or stupidity when I see it? Screw that!

"Listen, I want you fuckers to try something different for me today. I want you to start *thinking*. I want you to drop the God bullshit; the sexism; the racism; the nationalism; the greed. I want you to cut the shit and act like human beings today. Can you do that? I want you to examine what the fuck you're doing and why. Don't pull scams. Just start being nicer. Can you do that, just a little bit?"

Crime rates in the City started to go down.

"I call that a success," Mister Negative said on the air. "If only more of you really wanted the truth. Honesty is the best policy? Don't make me laugh. We all know how true that one is. 'You're ugly, with bad breath. You're fat and boring. You're an evil bitch, and I hate you.' If you said what you thought, you wouldn't make it through half your day without being arrested or murdered.[2] And if you call that 'best', you're an idiot. No, diplomacy is called for. My wife recently reminded me of that. The question is when. The answer is when *you* judge it to be. Don't let anyone tell you otherwise.

"I'm tired of being told I should take shit and like it, suck it up, be grateful for a body that doesn't work on a planet that occurred randomly (and doesn't work) in a universe that doesn't give a flying fuck more about me than about the ant on the sidewalk. Face it: this life is mostly bullshit, pain, and suffering, and I'm supposed to like it? What is wrong with you? Why on Earth are you telling me, 'If you don't have something nice to say, don't say anything at all'? How

---

[2] "Hours in which honesty is permitted have become rare . . . "
—Friedrich Nietzsche, *The Gay Science*

about, 'If we deal with everything honestly, we can actually work to make it better, but admitting the problems is the first step,' assholes? Your bullshit fantasyland is the biggest problem of all! Your bullshit fantasyland is the reason the problems continue! As my libertarian friends say, you don't have a right not to be offended. As George Orwell said, the right to free speech means the right to say things that are unpopular, because popular things hardly need protecting.[3]

"I really wonder what is wrong with those of you who are so anesthetized that you can't handle reality, that you cry—cry!—over not getting the personalized license plate you wanted. If you are really that fragile, then I suppose it's no wonder you can't handle anything more serious than that, in which case it is *you* who should hide at home every day, because you are the emotional infant, not me," he concluded his show that day.

"I don't give a shit about your money, your fancy vehicle, your fancy clothes, your fancy anything. I think your kids are ugly and stupid. Actually, I pity them, because your whole value system is fucked, and you are raising them to think and value what you do. I live in a country where one major political party's reason for being is the position 'I resent being forced to help my fellow human beings.' Are you kidding? You should be ashamed of yourselves! At best, you think throwing money at a problem absolves you of caring about whether the money did any good. Why don't you just do the World a favor and drop dead? This means you, America. You know, the rest of the

---

[3] "If liberty means anything at all, it means the right to tell people what they do not want to hear."—George Orwell, preface to *Animal Farm*

World doesn't buy it. They might envy your wealth, but they spit on your morality, which says that it's okay to rape the planet, conquer and kill indiscriminately, and let our children clean up the mess. And so do I.

"This whole idea of national borders, of attaching resources and emotions to lines on a map, is retarded. (I'm sorry: did I say something wrong? Political correctness is an intellectual straitjacket, I'm sorry to have to inform you.) We need to get past the present of national borders to the future of 'One Earth'. We are all from Earth. Once we get rid of these lines on the map, we can celebrate both what we have in common and what we do not. I am a citizen of the World who happened to be born in one place; our resources and liberties should not be determined by where we are born. In some places, death immediately follows birth. That is wrong. Let's do away with that instead of wasting more money on things we don't need: war, tax cuts, and stuff.

"If you look at the Globe, you will immediately notice that some governments govern larger land areas than were ever governed by single governments before. This is due not only to technology but increased cooperation. This process will continue, yielding fewer and fewer governments until there are three, then two, then one. Think of the waste of resources and effort all these duplicate administrations cost us, how much we will be able to devote to working together for a change, instead of wasting ourselves on petty internal squabbles. If you think that makes me a nut, then Gene Roddenberry was a nut too—because that is what *Star Trek* is all about: one Earth united with no money anymore.

Don't like it? Get over it, because the writing's on the wall, and there's nothing you can do to stop it.

"Of course, now that I think about it, we live on a planet where babies are placed in garbage cans, so never mind. I'm back to 'you all suck'.

"Mister Negative," he said. "Strong as a skunk. Thanks for seeking the spray. Signing out."

The switchboard lit up, but Neg took off his earphones. Despite his colleagues rising in confusion and calling after him, he walked out and went home. The next day, he called the station to say that he was resigning his position.

After that, Neg sold his house and took his family into the country to farm. Living off the land, he found he was even happier than when he faced and pointed out human failings every day. Sometimes we have to take care of ourselves too.

With his wife's help, Neg even tried to be less mean. It was a matter of picking and choosing his battles carefully for his own (and his family's) benefit, too—Neg didn't want a mob of angry villagers coming after him with torches and pitchforks, and neither did those who cared about him.

But how did the City fare without him? That was up to its citizens . . . like you.

"Mister Negative" Afterword

This story is significant for a reason related to my development as a writer.

Since at least 1994, I had heard the injunction "show don't tell" and rejected it. I love exposition, and I think human beings sometimes do not appreciate that exposition is occasionally necessary, even desirable. "Usually show, sometimes tell," is more accurate and better advice, but of course it is subtler, more complex, and therefore harder to understand and to say. Regardless, that was and is my position.

However, in this case, on April 21 I wrote the following section of exposition and added it to the story:

> For decades, Mister Negative had faced misunderstanding and consequent overreaction to his simplest pronouncements. "It's not your fault if you're misunderstood," said one of his more sympathetic university friends, because she knew he had made every effort to be as clear and context-specific as possible. If he said what you were doing was foolish, that did not mean he said you were a fool overall; he was commenting on the one specific thought, word, or deed, nothing more. Humanity's propensity to generalize never ceased to confound him.

This propensity of Humanity's to misunderstand and overreact had caused Mister Negative to lose family members, friends, and acquaintances, sometimes he didn't even know when or why. They would just stop talking to him, stop acknowledging his efforts to soothe their feelings, stop treating him morally, block him from their lives.

This propensity of Humanity's to misunderstand and overreact had also caused his wife to lose friends, friends who took offense from his slightest condemnations of their religions, philosophies of government, or tastes in food. They would treat him cruelly as well.

He understood that these family, friends, and acquaintances were all in the wrong; they did not.

Their mistreatment led Mister Negative to suffer all manner of disappointment in Humanity, even outrage at being shunned for what he considered to be harmless comments. He continually had to settle for the consolations that they were not his fault or his loss. If someone was so sensitive as to be unable to handle even the slightest criticism, he felt sorry for that person, ultimately. However, it must be admitted that he was tired of being abused by those who did not understand or react appropriately. Even his patience had a limit.

His wife, Plus, was tired of being caught in the middle, but she bore it Stoically. There was a long list of so-called "friends" who continued to speak with her but not him, evidently because they could not handle the truth, even when the truth he delivered was in response to their questions or comments. *If you don't like the truth, you shouldn't seek it*, he concluded. And so those particular persons, even those who had asked for it, stopped seeking it from him. He pitied them.

"The truth hurts," the World said.

"The lie hurts," he said. "The truth heals."

Upon reading the story again with fresh eyes a day or two later, I immediately realized that this section added nothing to the story that was not already there, that it brought all forward momentum to a halt in a bad way. I took it right back out, except, of course, for the last two lines. These were things I would have liked to say (and some I had already said elsewhere in the story), but I concluded that it would be far better when writing a story to say such things in the context of the action, rather than dragging the reader away from what interests him or her: the story, the plot, the momentum. If I could find an appropriate place to work it in, great. If not, then not.

So really, it depends. But it took me until this story to see there were times when exposition could be a drag. Until this story I thought everyone else was a drag on literary inspiration.

About the Author

"A public service announcement for anyone who has only known Rob for two minutes or so: Rob is made of contrary atoms. Whatever makes perfect sense to you, he will immediately (and with surprisingly little indication of artifice or irony) assert the opposite. Does he really believe what he says? Probably, because he's made of contrary atoms. Will it do any good to argue? Probably not, but sometimes you are compelled to do so, because his assertions seem so patently unfounded and indefensible. Has he really thought it through? Hard to say, because he will defend it to the death no matter what. I for one celebrate the contrary atoms of Rob. Who's with me?"

—James Lee Phillips, friend of Robert since 1985

Robert Peate (1970 -) was born in Smithtown, New York, was graduated from Oswego High School in 1987, and was awarded his BA in Psychology by the State University of New York at Stony Brook in 1992. In 2006 a photograph he took of the Ambassador Hotel appeared on the *Oprah Winfrey Show*, and in 2010 his article "Are Times Hard, or Are We?" appeared in the *Oregon English Journal*. That same year he became a high-school English teacher and accepted a teaching position on the island of Saipan. He currently lives with his wife and two children in Oregon City, Oregon, where he continues to write.

"This above all: to thine own self be true,
And it must follow, as the night the day,
Thou canst not then be false to any man."

—William Shakespeare

"Tact is overrated."

—Moushumi Ghose

15016957R00061

Made in the USA
Charleston, SC
13 October 2012